W9-CBR-674

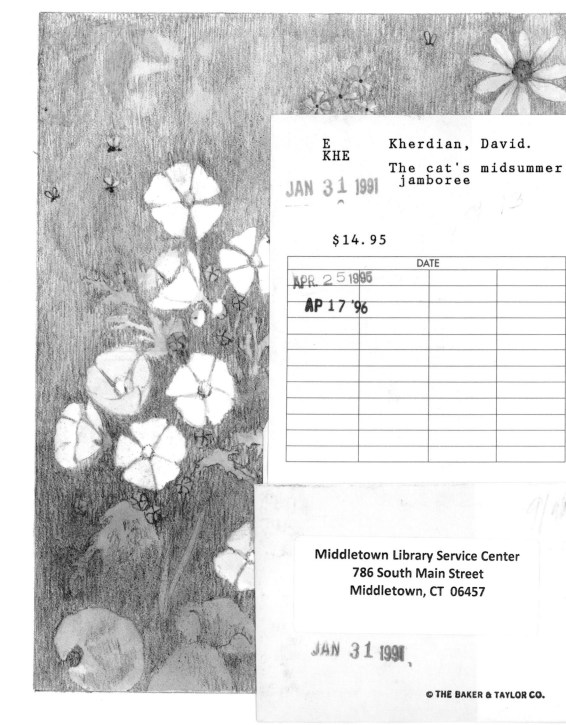

E
KHE

Kherdian, David.

The cat's midsummer jamboree

JAN 31 1991

$14.95

DATE			
APR. 25 1995			
AP 17 '96			

The Cat's Midsummer Jamboree

The Cat's Midsummer JAMBOREE

by David Kherdian and Nonny Hogrogian

Philomel Books   New York

Text and illustrations copyright © 1990 by David Kherdian and Nonny Hogrogian.
Published by Philomel Books, a division of The Putnam & Grosset Group.
200 Madison Avenue, New York, NY 10016. All rights reserved.
Published simulaneously in Canada.
Printed in Hong Kong by South China Printing Co. (1988), Ltd.
Book design by Nonny Hogrogian.

Library of Congress Cataloging-in-Publication Data
Kherdian, David. The cat's midsummer jamboree.
Summary: A roaming mandolin-playing cat encounters a number of other
musical animals on his travels, and the result is a jamboree in a tree.
[1. Animals—Fiction.   2. Music—Fiction] I. Hogrogian, Nonny.
II. Title.   PZ7.K527Cat 1990   [E]   89-16227   ISBN 0-399-22222-7
First impression

To Tessie

There once was a cat who loved to sing.
Strumming his mandolin,
he would roam and sing,
and romp and sing,
and dance and sing.

One day, to his surprise,
he came upon a toad
playing an harmonica
in the cavity of an old oak tree.

"Why do you hide your music?" asked the cat.
"Only the old oak branches
and the old oak trunk
can hear your playing."

"I don't need to be seen,
and I don't care if I'm heard,"
answered the toad.
"I just like to play for myself."

"That is how it is with me," the cat said.
"But your music is pleasing to my ear,
and if you were to join me we would
make a duet.
And a duet is worth going on the road with."

"That would certainly be different,"
answered the toad, and together they went.

It wasn't long before they heard a sound
coming from a meadow of ferns,
and peering around a tree,
they saw a fox tooting his flute.

"What are you doing out there by yourself?"
asked the cat.
"I'm playing my song," answered the fox.

"But your music is so good to hear,"
the cat replied, "and if you will join us
we will make a trio.
And a trio is worth traveling with."

"I think I will," answered the fox,
and all together they went.

They were playing so loud,
and so happily and so proudly,
that they danced right by a badger
banging his drum.

"Hey, you—and you, and you!" exclaimed the badger.
"Didn't you hear me keeping time to the music
with my drum? I heard you coming long before
I could see what you were."

"We're a trio," the cat replied proudly.
"What are you doing up there on your mound,
beside your hole,
all by your lonesome self?"

"Banging away, as everyone can see,"
the badger replied.
"So bang on your drum to accompany our tune,
and then we will be a quartet," said the cat.

The badger answered the cat, "I will be happy
to keep the beat and march out ahead."
And that's what he did,
and together they went.

They heard a melody drifting over the hill.
The cat stopped and pointed in the direction
of the sound being made by a violin,
that they now could see was being
played by a skunk.

"Why don't you join us?" asked the cat,
"because if you do we will make a quintet."

"I will," said the skunk,
"but you mustn't go too fast,
and you can't play so loud
that my violin won't be heard."

And so off they went,
a ringing quintet,
slow enough to be heard
if anyone wished to hear.

While crossing over a log
in the middle of a pond,
they spotted a goose playing a bassoon.
"I don't think the fish can hear you,"
said the cat, "and no one else is around,
so why don't you join us and we'll have a sextet."

"Six is my lucky number,"
answered the goose,
"and that's the only excuse
I think I will need."

And so the badger took the lead,
and the goose brought up the rear,
and off they all went.

They came to a tree at the edge of a meadow,
and there, high in its branches,
a raccoon could be seen—and heard—
playing an accordion.
The cat called up, "Come with us,
and we will have a jamboree."
"If you come up here," the raccoon answered,
"our music will carry to all who wish to hear."

And that's what they did,
and as the raccoon predicted,
they were heard far and near.

And so the musicians became
a jamboree in a tree.
And others came from far and from near,
players and listeners,

and cheerers and revelers,
and acrobats and jugglers,
until the world of that place
was filled with the happiness

that all began with a cat
who loved to sing.